W9-BJU-962

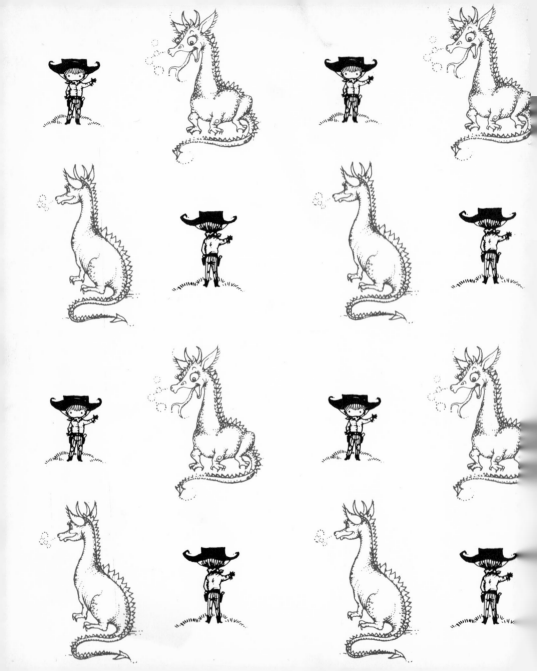

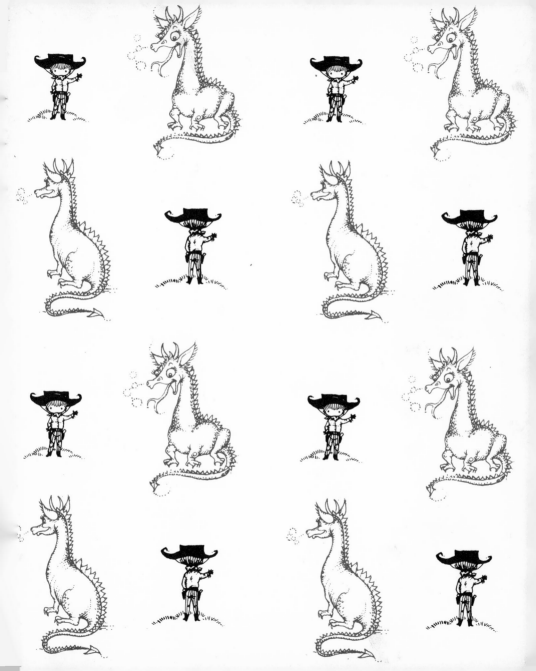

COWBOY'S SECRET LIFE

COWBOY'S SECRET LIFE

JOAN WALSH ANGLUND

HARCOURT, BRACE & WORLD, INC., NEW YORK

For the Cowboy's sister, Joy

Once there was a cowboy...

who led a very special life.

Every morning he would walk downstairs...

wait for his bus...

and go to school.

Every day he did his lessons...

hurried home...

and played with his toys.
　　Sometimes he raced on his scooter...

or played on his drum...

or chased the cat.

Sometimes he went shopping
with his mother...

or watched his fish . . .

or cleaned the yard.

Some days it rained...

and some days it snowed.

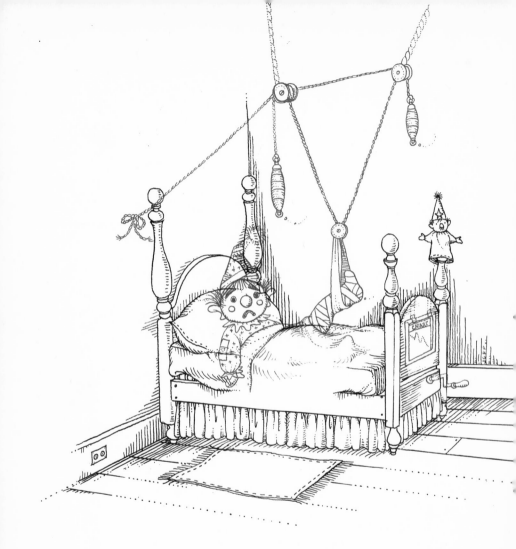

Sometimes he was busy...

and sometimes he was lazy....

But whether it was summer, winter, spring, or fall,
the cowboy led a very special life...
and he was happy!